Fussy Heron

A Fable by La Fontaine
Retold by Beverley Randell
Illustrations by Mini Goss

Rigby®
A Harcourt Achieve Imprint

www.Rigby.com
1-800-531-5015

Heron walked into the river and looked down.

"I like looking at myself in the water," he said to an old green frog. "I am very beautiful."

"Yes," said Heron,
"I am the best bird
in the river.
So I am going to eat
the best **fish**
in the river."

Heron saw some big fish
with spots.
"I can't eat fish with **spots!**"
he said. "They are not
the best fish in the river."

So he let the fish
swim away.

Heron saw some tiny fish. "They are **too little**," he said. "They are not the best fish in the river."

So he let the tiny fish swim away.

Heron said,

"I am getting very hungry.

Where can I find

the best fish in the river?"

The old green frog said,
"Heron, you are too fussy!
You let the best fish
swim away."

"Oh dear," said Heron.
"Now all the fish have gone,
and I will have to eat
this little **snail**!"

The old green frog saw Heron
eating the little snail,
and he laughed and laughed.